ACADEMY OF DANCE

DANCE TEAM BULLY

written by
Margaret Gurevich

illustrated by
Claire Almon

STONE ARCH BOOKS
a capstone imprint

Academy of Dance is published by Stone Arch Books,
A Capstone Imprint
1710 Roe Crest Drive
North Mankato, Minnesota 56003
www.mycapstone.com

Library of Congress Cataloging-in-Publication Data
Names: Gurevich, Margaret, author. | Almon, Claire, illustrator.
Title: Dance team bully / by Margaret Gurevich ; illustrated by Claire Almon.
Description: North Mankato, Minnesota : an imprint of Stone Arch Books,
[2018] | Series: Academy of Dance | Summary: Ms. Marianne's Academy
of Dance is Grace's refuge from middle school, but when Ella, the girl who
makes fun of her at school, decides to join the Academy, Grace has two
choices—let Ella's snide comments mess up her dance practice, or find
her voice and, with the support of her friends, stand up to the bully.
Identifiers: LCCN 2018002683| ISBN 9781496562036 (hardcover) |
ISBN 9781496562074 (pbk.)
Subjects: LCSH: Dance schools—Juvenile fiction. | Middle schools—Juvenile
fiction. | Bullying—Juvenile fiction. | Friendship—Juvenile fiction. | New
Jersey—Juvenile fiction. | CYAC: Dance teams—Fiction. | Middle schools—
Fiction. | Schools—Fiction. | Bullying—Fiction. | Friendship—Fiction. |
New Jersey—Fiction.
Classification: LCC PZ7.G98146 Dan 2018 | DDC 813.6 [Fic]—dc23
LC record available at https://lccn.loc.gov/2018002683

Designer: Kay Fraser

Printed and bound in Canada.
PA020

TABLE OF CONTENTS

CHAPTER 1

School Blues

I sit in social studies and watch the girls around me. They all have perfectly styled hair. Their bags all have fancy brand-name labels. I glance at my own beat-up messenger bag and try to focus on whatever our teacher, Ms. DiSousa, is saying.

"Nice hair, Grace," Ella Hayes hisses from behind me.

I seriously doubt her words are meant as a compliment. Last year, as Ella was leaving the nail salon, she spotted me leaving the Salvation Army across the street. She's made fun of my hair and clothes ever since.

Unlike Ella's perfectly straight, shiny red hair, my curly blond hair can be frizzy. My mom works like crazy, but I know we don't have the money for me to go to a fancy salon or buy expensive hair products. I usually wear a headband to keep my hair in check.

For my competitive tap dance team, I just twist it into a bun. It's not the most glamorous look, but at Ms. Marianne's Academy of Dance, *everyone's* hair is messy after two hours of sweating.

I guess I should be grateful Ella's never seen me like that. And at least she mocks me out of earshot of everyone else at school.

I glance at the clock. Ten minutes until I can leave for dance. Dance is the only good thing about Wednesdays.

Ms. DiSousa turns back to the board, and Ella kicks my chair. "Sorry," she says.

I doubt it was an accident. But knowing Ella, she'd insist it was if I tried to bring it up to a teacher. Not that I haven't thought about doing that. But it's not worth it. It would just make things worse.

I sigh under my breath and try to focus on Ms. Marianne's. The dance school is my happy place. None of the other dancers go to Truman Middle School with me. None of them know I don't quite fit in here. At Ms. Marianne's, no one cares that my leotards are a bit faded or a little too big. The girls on my dance team only care that I can move my tap shoes like lightning.

I place my homework in my binder and get ready to bolt. Three. Two. One. *Riiing!* I zoom out the door.

* * *

From the outside, Ms. Marianne's Academy of Dance is just a tiny brick building. The inside is another story. Studios line the hallway. When it's sunny, the rooms are bright with natural light. At night, overhead ceiling lights brighten the rooms.

I walk to the office first to say hi to the receptionist—also known as my mom. I love having her here. The truth is, I'm here because of her. We're only able to afford lessons at Ms. Marianne's because of extra office work Mom does in exchange for my dance tuition and costumes.

"How was school, kid?" Mom asks. She brushes her curly blond hair from her eyes.

I shrug and force a smile. "Same old. Happy to be here."

I haven't told my mom about Ella. She doesn't need the stress.

It's just the two of us, and I know she's tired enough with all the hours she works. I help when I can by taking care of stuff around the house or taking the bus to and from Ms. Marianne's instead of making Mom leave work to drive me.

She hugs me. "I'm happy you're here too."

"Have you seen Jada, Gabby, or Brie?" I ask, looking around for my closest friends on the dance team.

Mom laughs. "They were in here ten minutes ago asking about you."

I smile for real now. I love tap dance, which I have Monday, Thursday, and Saturday afternoons, but Wednesdays are even better. That's when I have all-team ballet.

No matter their dance specialty, all the dancers at Ms. Marianne's are required to take ballet. It strengthens our muscles and helps with flexibility.

Ballet is harder for me than tap, but since Jada, Gabby, Brie, and I all specialize in different dances, it's the only time we have class together.

And lately, with school being less fun than ever, seeing my best friends is everything.

CHAPTER 2

BALLET PRACTICE

I rest my left leg on the ballet barre, move my chest to my knee, and cradle my toes in my hands. It is a deep stretch and feels good after a long day of seventh grade. The truth is, every day is a long day at Truman.

At Ms. Marianne's, all my worries seem to float away. Here, it's just me and the dance floor.

I place my left leg on the floor and move my right foot to the barre, repeating the stretch.

"Hey, girl," Jada says, walking into the studio. She's wearing a turquoise leotard and ballet slippers, her usual dance clothes since ballet is her specialty. "How's it going?"

"Always better once I'm here," I say, grinning.

Jada only moved to New Jersey a few months ago, but we've gotten very close. Still, as close as I am to Jada and my other friends here, no one knows about Ella. I totally trust them, but I don't want to bring all that negative energy into my happy place.

"I hear you," says Jada. Her heels touch, and she bends her knees as she lowers herself into a *plié*.

"Brie and Gabby in the house," Gabby half-shouts, half-sings as she and Brie walk into the room. Brie blushes. Even though she always looks fierce and confident onstage during her hip-hop routines, she hates to be the center of attention.

They join us at the barre and begin moving their feet into the five ballet positions as the rest of the dancers filter in.

Ms. Marianne arrives at exactly four o'clock. The school has different teachers for the other dance specialties, but Ms. Marianne teaches all the ballet classes herself. "Good afternoon, ladies," she says. "We will begin with our feet positions."

We line up with partners. As usual, Gabby and Brie partner up; Jada and I do the same. I can hear Gabby talking about her *abuela* wanting her to learn how to cook. Brie chats about a vacation her dads are planning.

I move to sixth position, my feet parallel to each other, and practice stepping out to the side and forward. It's a basic step but something I need to practice. Keeping feet parallel is important in most tap moves and jumps, and it's something I forget to do when focusing on a new step.

Next to me, Jada practices fifth position. It's a harder move, but she easily touches the toes of one foot to her opposite heel.

I work on my knees next, bending them until my heels lift off the ground. This helps me remember to bend my knees in tap. Dropping a heel with bent knees is easier than with straight legs.

"When are you finally going to take up ballet?" Jada teases.

Some girls specialize in more than one dance, but tap is enough for me. "And upstage you?" I tease back. "I'll let you shine."

Jada laughs.

I raise myself up on my toes to strengthen my calves and heels, then lower back down. The concentration necessary for ballet bores me, but I'm thankful for it when tap class rolls around. Ballet helps me have better balance in tap.

"Water break," calls Ms. Marianne.

Brie, Gabby, Jada, and I grab our water bottles and huddle together.

"Is it just me," asks Brie, "or does class seem especially long today?"

"Not just you," says Gabby. "I want my jazz shoes!"

Jada pouts. "You guys say the same thing every week."

I throw my arm around Jada. "Maybe we can convince Ms. Marianne to make each of our dances a requirement too." I wink.

Jada chokes on her water. "No thanks. Ballet is more my speed. Concentrating on this helps take my mind off everything else."

I nod. "When I'm here, nothing else matters."

CHAPTER 3

BAD SURPRISE

The next day after school, I run to catch the bus. It lets me off half a mile from Ms. Marianne's and right in front of Sunny's Secondhand Shop. Mom and I have been shopping here for years. It's a great place to get dance supplies. Brand-new stuff can be pricey.

I've been saving for new tap shoes. Sunny called yesterday to say someone brought in a pair in my size. Talk about good luck!

"Just the lady I've been waiting for," Sunny says when I walk in. Her wide smile matches her name and the cheery, bright-yellow walls of her store. She reaches behind the counter and sets a pair of tap shoes on the counter.

I quickly examine them. The heel and toe plates look barely worn. I try on the shiny black shoes and jump around on the floor. My heart soars when I hear the clear *click-clack* they make.

"Thank you!" I say.

"My pleasure, hon," Sunny says with a smile. "You know how much I love you guys."

She rings me up, and I place the shoes in my dance duffel bag before changing into my sneakers. Excited, I walk out of Sunny's store. I can't wait to use them in today's class.

* * *

When I get to Ms. Marianne's, I quickly change into my leotard, put on my new tap shoes, and store my duffel bag in a locker. Then I head to the front office.

"Check them out," I say to my mom. I do a little dance to show off my new shoes.

"Looking good," she says, grinning.

Not wanting to be late, I hurry down the hall to my studio. Most of the girls are already there doing warm-ups at the barre, talking, or tapping on the floor. Tap class always has a livelier vibe than ballet. The moves here are freer and quicker.

"Hi, ladies!" Ms. Anne, our instructor, calls as she enters the room. She flashes a bright smile.

"I have an announcement," she continues. "A new student will be joining us today. Her dance school closed a month ago. She tried out for our team this past weekend. She's finishing up in the locker room and will be here shortly."

I wonder what grade the new girl is in and what she's like. I was new last year, so I know how hard it can be. I make a mental note to introduce her to Gabby, Brie, and Jada.

As we wait, I stand on my left foot and brush my right foot forward and back across the floor. *Scuffle, scuffle.* I repeat the move. My right toe hits the floor behind me. *Toe, toe.*

I pause and take a sip of water as I see Ms. Anne wave someone in from the hallway.

"Class," says Ms. Anne, "please welcome our new student . . ." She taps her hands on her knees like a drumroll.

A loud rushing noise fills my ears. Despite the water, my mouth goes dry. My hands shake, and I wrap them tightly around my water bottle. I know what she's going to say. I knew the second I saw the red hair.

"Ella Hayes," Ms. Anne finishes.

CHAPTER 4

No More Safe Space

I keep my eyes closed for another second because I know the second I open them, I'll see Ella's green eyes shooting daggers at me. Then Ms. Anne claps her hands, and my eyes spring open. I make sure to look anywhere but at Ella.

"Let's begin our combination," says Ms. Anne.

"Ms. Anne," Ella says in a sweet voice I've never heard before, "I know Grace. Can I stand next to her?"

Ms. Anne's face lights up. "Of course! Just make sure you stay focused."

She winks at me, but I can't smile. I slowly put down my water bottle and try to focus on the combination.

"Now I get to see you all the time," Ella whispers in my ear when she gets to her spot.

"Lucky me," I mutter.

Ms. Anne starts the music, and my legs move in their memorized routine. *Scuffle, scuffle, toe, toe.* I follow with two ball-heel combinations, alternating touching the balls and heels of my feet to the floor.

Ella's feet get too close to mine, and I quickly jump back, afraid she'll step on my toes. She snickers.

Get out of my head! I think. *Focus!*

My favorite step, a wing, is next. I feel Ella next to me, watching. My feet move to the side, and the balls of my feet brush against the floor. My arms circle wide.

Jada always flaps her arms like a bird when I do this move. I smile thinking about it. The funny image calms me and makes it easier to ignore Ella.

I rock back on my heels for a heel stand and hold the position. It's not easy to balance, so I'm proud of myself for holding the move.

"Not bad," hisses Ella. I lose my concentration and stumble.

"Keep going, Grace," calls Ms. Anne. "You got this!"

Except I don't. Not today. And if Ella is a permanent addition to my dance team, I don't know if I'll be able to *get it* ever again.

* * *

That night, I push the pasta around on my plate and hope my mom doesn't notice. Of course, she does.

"What's up?" Mom asks.

"Tough practice," I say. I force myself to eat a few noodles.

"Even with your cool new shoes?" she asks, smiling.

I want to cry thinking about how excited I was about the shoes. That feels like a lifetime ago compared to how awful I feel now. I nod, afraid if I speak I'll start bawling.

"I've seen you master tons of moves in a short time." Mom squeezes my hand. "I have faith in you."

"Thanks," I whisper. I used to have faith in myself too. I need to get that back. I need to get my mind focused back on my feet and off Ella Hayes.

I eat a few more noodles for fuel and walk down the hallway to the den to practice. *You can do this,* I tell myself.

Scuffle, scuffle, toe, toe. My feet move quickly, and I smile at the happy *click-clack* sound. Next I shift to the ball-heel combos and wings. I wave my arms extra wide and add more energy. I end with a heel stand and hold the move for a count of ten.

Yes! I cheer silently. I close my eyes to savor the moment.

Suddenly Ella's face looms behind my eyelids. I open my eyes and sigh heavily. I know I can't let her ruin my safe place, but I don't know how.

CHAPTER 5

FROM BAD TO WORSE

At school the next day, I doodle pictures of tap shoes in my notebook while I wait for Ms. DiSousa to begin.

"Fun class yesterday, right?" says Ella, nudging my shoulder.

I don't look at her. "Yep."

"Looked like you had some trouble with the heel stand," Ella continues, sounding less than sincere. "That's too bad."

I suck in air through my teeth and press my pen hard against the paper.

She smirks. "I wouldn't want to talk about it either."

"What made you choose Ms. Marianne's anyway?" I ask. I need to know.

"Not my first choice, but my mom likes how close it is. That school is lucky to have me. *I* don't fumble *my* heel stands." She laughs and takes her seat before I can respond.

Ms. DiSousa starts talking about the clothing styles of the 1700s, and I look around the classroom. The girl in front of me, Olivia, is wearing jeans with a designer label on the back. Next to me, another classmate, Maddie, taps her manicured nails on her desk and absently plays with the charm on her gold bracelet.

I do my best with clothes, but my stuff isn't nearly as nice as what the other girls wear. Today, I'm wearing one of my favorite outfits: a soft pink sweater, stretchy jeans, and shoes with chunky heels.

It's all from Sunny's. Sunny even found a necklace with a pink heart charm that goes perfectly with the sweater, but, as I look around, I feel out of place.

When the bell rings, Ella takes her time gathering her books. My heart beats quickly because I know she's waiting for me.

"I guess I'll see you tomorrow," Ella says when we're at the door.

"Right," I mumble.

"By the way, that sweater is one of your better finds. You almost can't tell it wasn't good enough for anyone else." She laughs and pushes past me as tears sting my eyes.

* * *

On Saturday, I hang in the hallway with Brie, Jada, and Gabby. We're all waiting for our dance classes to start.

They haven't met Ella yet—she started after Wednesday's all-team class—and I haven't told them about her. But when I see Ella exiting the locker room, I know that's about to change.

"Hi, Grace," Ella says when she spots us.

My palms get sweaty. I can't pretend I didn't hear her with my friends watching. I slowly wave hello.

She comes over. "I'm Ella," she introduces herself. "I just joined the tap dance team." Her smile hides how mean she is.

"You dance with Grace?" asks Jada. She looks from me to Ella.

"Uh-huh. We go to the same school too!"

Gabby, Brie, and Jada stare at me. They must be wondering why I didn't mention her before.

"Classes, everyone!" calls Ms. Marianne.

I wave goodbye to my friends, and Jada mouths, "We'll talk later."

I desperately *don't* want to talk about it later. I already know it won't do any good. Ella never does anything when she knows other people are watching. But at the same time, I know I'll need my friends at my side if I'm going to get through this.

I focus on my warm-up and ignore Ella's attempts to distract me. *Ball, ball.* The balls of my feet tap the floor. *Heel, heel.* My heels beat a rhythm. *Toe, Toe.*

The sound of the plates against hardwood calms me, and I quicken my pace, repeating the whole combination. I add a quick ball change. I place my right foot behind me and rock on the ball of it while my left foot is off the ground. I repeat the same movement with the left foot behind me. Hearing my shoes *clacking* with each move reminds me why this is my safe place.

"Bravo, Grace!" Ms. Anne shouts above the music. "That's some fancy footwork!"

I grin and hear Ella grunt beside me. Her feet aren't moving as quickly as mine. My ankles are loose and ready as I wait for Ms. Anne to give us more instructions.

"Today we're adding a new move to our combination," our instructor says. "Two buffalos and two shuffles. Watch me."

Ms. Anne jumps on her right leg to start the buffalo. Then she brushes the floor twice with the ball of her left foot. *Click!* She jumps on the floor with her left foot and brings the right one up to cross at her left knee. She repeats the buffalo.

"And now the shuffles," she says. She brushes the ball of her right foot across the hardwood floor, then repeats the move with her left. "Put it all together!"

She completes two buffalos, followed by two shuffles. The room erupts with *clickety-clacks* as we all do the same.

"Nice job, ladies!" says Ms. Anne. "Way to go, Grace!"

"Way to go, Grace," Ella mimics under her breath.

I feel my stomach tightening and try to push away the sick feeling. *You've got this.*

"From the top!" Ms. Anne calls, turning to face the other side of the room.

We begin the combination from the very beginning. *Scuffle, scuffle, toe, toe. Wing.* My feet move to the side, and my arms circle wide. I lean back on my heels for the heel stand.

Ella shifts closer, and I start the buffalo before she can knock me down. I jump on my right foot, then brush the floor twice with the toe of my left foot.

My heels stay off the ground, just like Ms. Anne demonstrated minutes before. I repeat the move, then move my toes forward and back across the floor for the shuffles.

Suddenly Ella bumps me—hard. I fall to the floor, and my face reddens. Ms. Anne turns around to see what happened.

"So sorry!" Ella exclaims. I can tell by her satisfied expression that she doesn't mean it. But Ms. Anne can only hear Ella's voice. She can't see her face.

"No, you're not!" I hiss back.

Ella shrugs. "Not all of us can be as good as you." She glares at my tap shoes. "Maybe whoever threw those away sprinkled them with magic fairy dust first."

I pick myself up and turn away from Ella. Seconds ago, I was so proud of myself. How does Ella steal my confidence every time?

CHAPTER 6

CONFESSIONS

After practice, Brie, Jada, Gabby, and I sit on the soft blue carpet of Jada's bedroom. They all wanted the details on Ella. I've just finished recapping our latest run-in for them.

"But wait," says Jada. "I still don't get why she picks on you."

I stare at my hands. I haven't told them about the Salvation Army store run-in or how I don't fit in with the girls at my school.

"C'mon," says Gabby, gently bumping me with her shoulder, "you can tell us anything."

I bite my lip. They like me. They're my friends. "She saw me coming out of the Salvation Army store once," I say quietly.

No one says anything.

"So . . . what?" Brie finally asks.

"So," I say, "she knows I shop there. No one at my school would be caught dead there. All the other girls at my school get their nails done, they all have new clothes, you know . . ." My voice trails off.

Gabby throws her hands up in the air. "Are you serious? I get hand-me-downs from my cousins all the time. Who cares?"

How come they don't see this as a big deal? Maybe they don't get it.

"My tap shoes are from Sunny's Secondhand Shop," I say quietly. "Most of my stuff is. We can't really afford new stuff." I raise my head to look at them.

"That jerk!" cries Jada. "Who cares where you get your clothes or how much money your family has?"

"Exactly!" says Brie. "That's just crazy. Someone at my school once said something rude about me having two dads. People are dumb."

"This isn't OK," says Gabby, slamming her fist on the carpet. "We love you, Grace. And I love your tap shoes."

"And I love your hair," says Jada.

"And I love your face," Brie adds, laughing.

I laugh too. "Thanks, guys. I just . . . I don't know how to stop her from getting to me."

"We won't let her," Gabby says firmly.

"Agreed," Brie says. "You are too good of a dancer to let her in your head."

CHAPTER 7

OFFBEAT

For the rest of the weekend I think about what my friends said. It felt good to finally tell them and to know they have my back. I replay what Brie said too: "You are too good of a dancer to let her in your head."

On Monday, I avoid Ella at school. I have my books ready so I can walk into class just as it's about to begin and zoom out the second it ends.

When I get to Ms. Marianne's after school, my head is clearer than it's been all week. I change into a black leotard and my tap shoes and look at myself in the mirror.

You can do this, I tell myself. I take a deep breath. Then I hear Ella's voice in the hallway, and my palms get sweaty. *Shake it off. Don't let her in your head.*

But I can't seem to do it. Everything looks wrong. My leotard looks more faded than it did seconds ago. I notice pieces of hair sticking out from my bun. Even scuff marks I'd barely noticed on my tap shoes now seem to flash at me like hazard lights. I grab my water and run out of the locker room before Ella can get there.

I think about asking Ms. Anne for a new spot in the routine, but I don't know what reason I would give. I hate that the place I love has turned into a prison.

I try to focus on the shiny floor, the barre, the large mirrors, and the giant window. I practice basic tap moves, *toe and heel, toe and heel,* just to get the *cloppity-clop* sounds in my head.

Before my mom started working here last year, I would watch YouTube videos of tap dancers nonstop and practice moves on our kitchen floor. Sometimes the local Y offered free dance workshops, and I took those.

I've come a long way since then, I remind myself. *I'm on the dance team! Why am I letting Ella take all that away from me?*

I practice the combination in front of the mirror and feel calmer. I tune out the voices around me and focus on the *click-clack-clop* of my tap shoes. My feet brush against the floor faster and faster.

Then, out of nowhere, someone shoves me hard from behind. I stumble.

"You should really pay attention to where you're practicing," says Ella slyly.

Furious, I whip around. I've tried ignoring Ella at school, but that hasn't worked.

My mouth is dry, but I swallow and find my voice. "What is your problem?" I ask.

The words don't come out strong like I'd imagine in my head. My voice is weak and shaky.

Ella laughs and shakes her head. She pulls at my leotard. "You really need to find clothes that fit."

I know my friends are right about clothes and money not mattering, but my mom has been working so hard to get me here. I feel tears forming in my eyes and can't stop them.

Ella looks satisfied and makes her way over to another section of the barre. Seeing me break down is what she's been wanting, but I can't let her win.

"And a one and a two," Ms. Anne's clear voice calls.

When did she come in? I wonder.

My head feels underwater. I try to move my feet—*scuffle, scuffle*—but I'm a second behind everyone else. I tap my toe on the floor, but everyone is a beat ahead. I can't get the rhythm back.

"Having problems?" Ella whispers, just loud enough for me to hear.

Tears slip out of my eyes. I can't take any more. I grab my water and run out of the studio.

CHAPTER 8

GETTING BACK THE GROOVE

"You're awfully quiet," Mom says that evening. We're watching our favorite show, *Dance Stars*. I can barely focus on the dancers.

I shrug. "Tired."

"You didn't wait for me to give you a ride home after class today," she says softly.

I feel the tears coming again and turn away.

Mom strokes my hair. "Is dance getting too hard? Is it interfering with school?" she asks.

I almost laugh. *No,* school *is interfering with the class,* I want to tell her. Instead I say, "It's none of those things."

I look at Mom's concerned face. We tell each other everything. I *want* to tell her about Ella. But what would she do about Ella anyway? What would happen in tap class, at my locker, at school? The problem isn't just at tap. It's everywhere. I need to stop being afraid so I can get her out of my head for good.

"I'm here for you if you want to talk," Mom tells me. Worry lines pucker around her mouth and eyes.

"I know," I say. My friends are here for me too. Now it's up to me to make a change.

* * *

On Wednesday, Ms. Marianne lets me come in early to practice before ballet. After Monday, I need to get my head back in the game.

"I thought I heard someone in here," says Ms. Anne, entering the studio. "How are you?"

I blush. I never explained just running out of class the other day. "I'm OK. I was having a rough day Monday. I'm sorry."

Ms. Anne cocks her head to the side. "We've all been there." She smiles. "Do you want to show me the combination now? I have time."

"Yes, please!" I beam.

I shake out my wrists and ankles and take a deep breath. Ms. Anne turns on the music. My right foot brushes forward and back across the hardwood floor. *Scuffle, scuffle.* I repeat the move with my left, then tap my toes. *Toe, toe.*

The familiar sounds fill my body, and I relax. The ball-heel combinations are next, and my feet quickly tap the floor, not missing a beat. The wings are next. The balls of my feet move to the side, brush the floor, then come back in. My arms circle to the sides like propellers.

"Looking great!" Ms. Anne calls above my tapping.

I grin and move easily into the heel stand. *One, two, three, four, five. Now for the end.* I jump on my right foot, then brush the floor with the ball of my left foot. *One, two.* I jump on my left foot and bring my right ankle to the left knee, then repeat the buffalo with my other leg.

I finish with the shuffles. My feet glide on the floor, making the best *click-clack* sound. This is my safe space again. Just me, the music, and my feet. No distractions.

"That was some fancy footwork," Ms. Anne says when I finish. "I've missed that smile."

I smile wider. "Me too."

I'm so happy that at first I don't even notice the time. But when I look at the clock and see that ballet starts in ten minutes, my stomach drops to the floor.

CHAPTER 9

FiNDiNG My VOiCE

Shaking, I walk slowly into the ballet studio. Brie, Gabby, and Jada immediately crowd around me.

Jada squeezes my shoulder. "You'll be fine," she says.

I nod and clutch my water bottle, but I'm too nervous to take a sip. I close my eyes and try to bring back the feeling I had with Ms. Anne minutes ago. My feet and I felt at home again.

Ella appears in the doorway in a sparkly, black leotard. "You going to finish class this time?" She smirks at me.

Jada steps in front of me. "Do you have a problem?" she asks.

Ella doesn't flinch. "Not with you."

"That's what you think," says Gabby. "We're all friends here."

Ella shrugs. "*Draaama*," she says before walking to the barre.

"I didn't mean to drag you guys into this," I say quietly.

Jada puts her arm around me. "Don't be silly. You didn't drag us into this. We're your friends. And she doesn't need to make trouble."

"Did you tell Ms. Anne? What did she say?" asks Brie.

"And your mom?" asks Gabby.

"She only does it when no one is watching, and I . . . didn't tell them." I lace my fingers together. "I've been hoping to deal with it on my own. I don't want to worry my mom."

"I get that," says Gabby. "But if she keeps bullying you, we should say something."

"We're here for you," says Brie.

I give her a hug as Ms. Marianne walks in. Then we all walk to the barre.

Ella moves over so she's near me. She waits until Ms. Marianne turns on the music before hissing in my ear, "Isn't it time for another leotard? I bet the Salvation Army has more."

I try to move away and practice my *pliés*. But Ella won't let it go. "*Soooo* sorry," she whispers, poking me in the side.

I look at Gabby, Brie, and Jada. Anger flashes in their eyes. I clench my fists. Ella doesn't get to ruin this school for me. My mom worked too hard to get me here.

Scooting even closer, Ella pushes me, and I stumble. "Must be the secondhand shoes," she says louder.

Tears push at my eyes, but they aren't going to stop me this time. I turn so fast, Ella loses her balance. "Enough," I say.

She's facing me now, nostrils flaring. "Are you saying those shoes aren't used?"

I take a deep breath. "So what if they are? They don't stop me from dancing. Neither does this leotard. The only thing stopping me is *you*." I don't realize I'm raising my voice until I notice girls gathering around us. "You," I say again, "are. Always. In. My. Face. I'm here to dance. What are *you* here to do?"

Ella sputters. She looks at the group.

Ms. Marianne speed-walks in our direction. "What's going on here?"

Ella is silent, but this time I'm not. "Ella won't leave me alone," I say. "She keeps making rude comments about my shoes and my dance clothes. And she just pushed me."

Now Ms. Marianne looks angry. "Is that true?" she asks, looking at us.

My friends nod. So do some of the other dancers who saw what happened. Ella glares at me, still not saying anything.

"This dance school is about respect, Ella," Ms. Marianne says. "Not about who's wearing what. If you can't respect that, I'm not sure this is the right school for you."

Ella snorts. "Whatever. I don't need this place!" she snaps. "I'm too good for this school anyway." She grabs her water and marches out of the studio.

I stare after her open-mouthed. "What just happened?" I whisper.

"You got your voice back," says Jada.

Ms. Marianne puts her hand on my shoulder. "How long has Ella been treating you this way?" she asks.

I shift my feet uncomfortably. "Always."

"I'm so sorry I didn't realize what was happening sooner. I never want my students to feel like you must have." Ms. Marianne hugs me.

"Thank you," I say.

"You did great," says Gabby.

"It helped knowing you are all here for me," I say.

Ms. Marianne turns on the music, and we all go back to the barre. I let the music fill me. I know I'll have to see Ella at school tomorrow, but I'm not scared anymore. I stood up to her once. I can do it again.

CHAPTER 10

NEW FRiENDS

On Thursday, I don't linger at my locker before going into class. I'm not going to put up with Ella's bullying anymore.

Here goes nothing, I think as I slide into my seat in Ms. DiSousa's room.

I don't have to spend much time wondering what's going to happen. Ella is by my desk almost immediately. Ms. DiSousa is still standing by the door and not looking in our direction.

"I'm so glad I'm done with your trashy dance school," sneers Ella.

"Me too," I say.

Ella frowns and turns her attention to my clothes. She pulls on my yellow sweater. "When are you going to get clothes that fit?"

My face turns red. *Don't let her get to you.* "I like my clothes."

She laughs. "Someone has to."

In front of me, Maddie spins around in her seat. Her bracelet charm jingles. "*I* like that sweater," she says, smiling. "Yellow looks really good on you."

I study her smile. It looks real and not like she's teasing me. "Thank you."

"Seriously?" Ella asks. "You know she got it at the Salvation Army or something, right?"

Maddie stands up. Her head only reaches Ella's ear, but that doesn't seem to bother her.

"Who cares?" She turns her back on Ella and faces me. "Have you ever been to Sunny's Secondhand Shop? I love that place."

My heart beats quickly. I look around the room as I realize something—I judged these girls based on what they were wearing. That's exactly what Ella did to me. But that ends now.

"I love that place too," I say.

"What are you guys talking about?" Olivia asks, glancing over at us.

"Sunny's," says Maddie. "Have you ever been there?"

Olivia shakes her head. "What is it?"

I take a deep breath and say, "It's a secondhand store. It sells previously worn clothing, but the stuff is all really cute and in great condition."

"Sounds cool," says Olivia, nodding. "Maybe I'll check it out."

Ella grits her teeth. Before she can say anything else, the bell rings and Ms. DiSousa walks into the room.

"Let's get back to studying the colonization of the Americas," she says.

Ella stomps to her seat, and Maddie sits back down in front of me. But then she turns around and taps her nails on her desk to get my attention. "Let's go check out Sunny's this week," she whispers as Ms. DiSousa turns to the SmartBoard.

"Awesome!" I say.

Ella mumbles something behind me, but that's all she says for the rest of the period. She doesn't kick my chair or poke me. When the bell rings to end the day, she grabs her books and rushes out.

I hug my books to my chest and walk to my locker. I see the students in the hallway in a new way. No one is staring at me or paying attention to what I'm wearing. Maybe they never did.

I grab my coat and backpack, adjust my headband, and step outside. The sun is shining, and I soak it in.

Tomorrow, Ms. Marianne's will be my happy place again. What's even better is that school won't be a place I dread anymore. No more clammy hands, no more stomach tied in knots, no more feeling bad about myself.

"See you later!" Maddie and Olivia call as they rush past me.

Days ago, I wouldn't have wanted to draw attention to myself. I would have wondered what they really thought of me.

Today, I shout back, "Later!"

I've finally found my voice, and I don't want to hold back anymore.

ABOUT THE AUTHOR

Margaret Gurevich is the author of many books for kids, including Capstone's *Gina's Balance, Aerials and Envy,* and the award-winning Chloe by Design series. She has also written for *National Geographic Kids* and Penguin Young Readers. While Margaret hasn't done performance dance since she was a tween, this series has inspired her to take dance classes again. She lives in New Jersey with her son and husband.

ABOUT THE ILLUSTRATOR

Claire Almon lives and works in Atlanta, Georgia, and holds a BFA in illustration from Ringling College of Art and Design, as well as an MFA in animation from Savannah College of Art and Design. She has worked for clients such as American Greetings, Netflix, and Cartoon Network and has taught character design at Savannah College of Art and Design. She specializes in creating fun, dynamic characters and works in a variety of mediums, including watercolor, pen and ink, pastel, and digital.

GLOSSARY

barre (BAR)—the horizontal wooden bar used by dancers for support and balance

combination (KAHM-buh-nay-shun)—in dance, a mixture or sequence of two or more patterns or movements or steps

dread (dred)—to fear greatly

loom (LOOM)—to appear in a large, strange, or frightening form, often in a sudden way

routine (roo-TEEN)—a part (as of an act or a sports performance) that is carefully worked out so it can be repeated often

secondhand shop (SEHK-uhnd-hand SHOP)—a store that buys or sells items that have already been owned or used, usually at a less-expensive price

sincere (sin-SEER)—trustworthy and genuine

sputter (SPUH-tur)—to speak quickly or in a confused way because you are upset, surprised, etc.

upstage (uhp-STAYJ)—to steal attention away from

TALK ABOUT IT!

1. Why do you think Ella was so focused on giving Grace a hard time, both at school and at dance? Talk about some possible reasons.

2. Do you think Grace should have told her mom or one of her teachers what was going on? How would you have handled the situation?

3. Bullying can be more than just mean—it can be dangerous. Talk about some ways to combat bullying if you see it happening.

WRITE ABOUT IT!

1. Grace realizes that she judged the other girls at her school, just like Ella did to her. Write about a time you judged someone before getting to know them. How did that person end up being different than you expected?

2. Brie, Jada, and Gabby all stand up for Brie. Write about a time a friend stood up for you or a time you stood up for a friend. How did it help or change the situation?

3. Ms. Marianne's Academy of Dance is Grace's safe space. Do you have a place that makes you feel safe and at home? Write about it! Explain what the place is and why it makes you feel good.

TAP DANCE STARS

Whether on-screen or onstage, a tap performance is an energetic experience that delights its audience. Here are some notable dancers who left their unique marks on the tap world!

Fred Astaire brought his signature tap style to big Hollywood movies of the 1930s–1950s. A handsome face and fancy footwork made Astaire an instant star; his work was the product of constant practice, though he made dancing look effortless. His tap routines are still cherished by the dance world. Astaire's career lasted many years, and he was awarded the American Film Institute's Lifetime Achievement Award in 1981.

Sammy Davis Jr. was a true entertainer—a singer, actor, and skillful tap dancer. He became famous as a member of the famous Rat Pack and was inducted into the Tap Dance Hall of Fame in 2005. Davis was among the very first African American artists to be supported by both Caucasian and African American audiences.

Gregory Hines was a celebrated tap dancer, musician, actor, and director. He studied dance from a young age and began a successful Broadway career in the 1970s. He later starred in numerous films and became a household name. In 1992, Hines won a Tony Award for Best Actor in a Musical.

Gene Kelly was another dancer who made the movies of the 1940s and 1950s come to life with his unique tap routines. Kelly even acted as choreographer and producer for some of the films he starred in. His most iconic scene is his rain-splashing dance from *Singin' in the Rain*, known to many as one of the best dance films ever made.

Ginger Rogers was Fred Astaire's partner in film and onstage. She was a dancer and an actress and shone as a talent alongside Astaire, as well as in her own right. In 1940, Rogers won the Academy Award for Best Actress in a Leading Role for her performance in *Kitty Foyle*. As a duo, Rogers and Astraire changed the popularity of tap dancing and musicals in America.

THE FUN DOESN'T STOP HERE!

DISCOVER MORE AT
WWW.CAPSTONEKIDS.COM